Awaken the As

MW01227680

Index

Introduction: Inspire

This book is to inspire those who feel like their lost from swimming in their pain, abused by someone they loved. Filling tortured by their own emotions. I wrote this book to share my testimony and once more to uplift your hearts I was in a tragic and dangerous marriage. This book talks about Gideon he was torn on his own emotions and so much more anxiety filling as if he's not strong enough or not good enough well the Lord brought him through it and made him the strongest bravest meanest craziest soldier that fought for God besides David and many more that fought by God's side. Then there is Meshack Shadrack and Bendigo they were just little boy's teenagers being bullied by another king because of their faithfulness of worshiping one God and not flesh of a man the Lord delivered them out of the pit of the fury furnish fire. This book is to awaken the asunder within you to find the soldier inside of your heart that God called you to be a brave warrior and undefeated for you are to be victorious. An overcomer.

Chapter 1: My Angel Watching Over Me

My dad did not like the man I met. He also saw something I did not see, but of course, I did not listen. I dated this man for about two years then I married him and moved to Cheyenne Oklahoma. But before we moved, I found out I was pregnant. probably two in half months maybe three months pregnant. I also had a four-year-old daughter. And of course, at this time I was running from the Lord and God started to put me through so many trials and battles to wake me up to realize what I got myself into. Just to clear the air I was in love with a junkie... People will ask all the time why does God allow things to happen to other people, I can answer that. Look at Gideon in Judges CH. 6 and CH. 7 and you will find where the

Israelite's would fall into doing their own thing so God would see they are disobedient and put his people through bondage and slavery just to get their attention. God chose Gideon to wake up his people and all because someone prayed and asked God to deliver the people so God got some body's attention. Well same with me God was trying to get my attention. At this time my husband was going through grief from his brother passing away and decided to rage at me as if I was a practice target. I was tormented and beaten, starved. Now my little 4 years old was also going through a hard time having to see her mother being tormented, used, abused, used as an experiment to practice on me for target practice. I started to notice God by my side I felt him with me... I begin to call upon God day after day. I did not stop calling after God day after day. God spoke me and said this, Go to your husband's father and mother figure's house you must walk there, with them they will provide shelter food and water go now you will make even with your daughter by your side it will be a long walk for you but I will be with you... It took me half of the day to get there to this place a place where God sent me, they love the Lord with all their hearts. When I got their I waited on their front door a comfortable chair they helped us with food, water and helped us on our feet and gave us shelter. Then one day we decided to move somewhere else after my new daughter was born and she was about 6 months old we both figured hey maybe if we try something else and move somewhere else everything will be okay. Things began to get worse, instead of better. We moved still in Oklahoma by sweet water, you ready for this...

I have no idea where we are at in the middle of nowhere, He decides to put a gun to my had, two-barrel shotgun. keeps me up day and night hardly any rest.

Been up mostly 42 hours starving no food or water. I watched him clean it up, I watched him load it up. Then he said to me your parents don't love you, I don't love you, and your kids don't love you... It was silent for a minute or two, just staring in each other's eyes, after two minutes passed he said any last words, I said yes I raised my hands towards the heavens and said My God Will Deliver Me Out OF This I lifted my head and closed my eyes and pulled the trigger and click, he said what and pulled the trigger again and click. He looked at his gun and said what is going on here then he heard a noise behind me, what was that? I said what was what? I felt the Lord behind me, without a shout of a doubt God sent an army to protect me. He started shaking, He said out loud someone is helping you, I said yes there is my God is with me, so why don't you go find him? He went looking for him it was quite and he came back looked at his gun opened it up the part that holds the bullets came towards me and try to punch me but couldn't, and the bullets were gone, he said what happened to my bullets? I said I don't know you had the gone the whole time all of the sudden we both hear footsteps on the front porch and I stayed but he went to the front door there he saw footprints all around the house. He came back and saw his bullets on the front porch. I saw him come in as I sat in the living room it is silent. Finally, I get to go to sleep. My body hurting from being beaten and starved but at the time all I cared about was getting rest with my kids.

Chapter 2: Tough Lesson I Learned

When we surrender our self's in a deep situation like this or any situation period God shows up, I'll show you the kind of show up I'm talking about. Let us look at Daniel CH. 3 really quick. IF you read it then you can understand of what I'm about to tell you but I courage you to go read, a king named Nebuchadnezzar built a statue and set it up in a place called Babylon and commanded that everyone worshiped this statute at a certain time of the day while the trumpets are blowing, well three men called Shadrach, Meshach, Abednego refused to bow down to another god to a statue. Everyone obeyed the law except these three teenagers. A servant of the king saw this and reported to King

Nebuchadnezzar. The king asked for these men to be brought to the king and asked them a question. Why did you not bow to the statue when the music was going? The three men answered to him and said we don't have to answer to you, Wee only worship one God and you are not a God. Then the king answered and said through them in the fire and turn up the fire so high so the guards did and the guard that threw the three men in the fire did burn except Rad-shack, Meshack, and Abednego the king shouted I thought I told you to throw three in the fire, the guard answered and said you did my lord and we did so. Well, the king saw four men in the fire the Lord was in the fire with them only the rope that bound them was burnt off and they did not get touched. The king saw who was in there and told them to get them out of the fire let them out. God will defend you as long as your heart is where you allow it to be with the Lord.

Psalms 91:1-7

1He that dwelleth in the secret place of the most; high shall abide under the shadow of the Almighty.

2 I will say of the Lord, He is my refuge and my fortress: my God; in him will I trust.

3 Surely, he shall deliver thee from the snare of the fowler, and from the noisome pestilence.

4 He shall cover thee with his feathers, and under his wings shalt thou trust: his truth shall be thy shield and buckler.

5 Thou shalt not be afraid for the terror by night; nor for the arrow that flieth by day; 6

Nor for the pestilence that walketh in darkness; nor for the destruction that waste at noonday.

7 A thousand shall fall at thy side, and ten thousand at thy right hand; but it shall not come nigh thee.

Psalms 91 is talking about trusting in God that he will protect you and if you were paying attention in verse 4 his truth shall be thy shield and buckler this verse means he will show you the truth and protect you from the lies that will blind you. That is what this VRS. did for me when I gave my life to the Lord my eyes were opened and I could see all the filth and lies that was brought a pone me.

Chapter3: If You Can Beat It You Can Defeat It

He can deliver you out of any situation possible if you let him, so surrender yourself unto our savior and he will deliver you out of any situation. Now it took me two years to get out of this situation and four years to completely delivered from the entire situation. I suffered P.T.S.D. that is post dramatic stress disorder. Every little thing bothered me I was always scared, confused, I always had to test the Lord and ask him if he was still there, Now if you know anyone who go's threw fear allow them to read this book that I wrote because this book will deliver them out of fear, or anxiety or even P.T.S.D. Fasting and praying a lot of it. To be honest with you I probably went every two weeks I would fast for a whole week. It was hard it was not easy this is not an easy battle to conquer but when you do it is the biggest triumph and testimony yet and many more to come, also pray like you never prayed before like your giving birth to a baby, shouting letting all your emotions and even your anger out. Pray about the person that hurt you, if you do this God will help you out of this hate, out this dungeon feeling of bondage. Listen If You Can Beat It, You Can Defeat IT, If You Can Defeat It Then You Can Be Delivered from It.

Chapter 4: What It Means Too Break Out Fear

Judges CH 6

1 And the children of Israel did evil in the sight of the Lord: and the Lord delivered them into the hand of Median seven years. 2 And the hand of Median prevailed against Israel: and because of the Midianites the children of Israel made them the dens which are in the mountains, and caves, and strongholds. 3 And so it was, when Israel had sown, that the Midianites came up, and the Amalekites, and the children of the east, even they came up against them; 4 And they encamped against them, and destroyed the increase of the earth, till thou come unto Gaza, and left no sustenance for Israel, neither sheep, nor ox, nor ass. 5 For they came up with their cattle and their tents, and they came as grasshoppers for multitude; for both they

and their camels were without number: and they entered into the land to destroy it. 6 And Israel was greatly impoverished because of the Midianites, and the children of Israel cried unto the Lord.

Note: Anyone who is lost in sin of this world can find a way to come to their senses when they decide to listen you don't listen well God will find a way to grab your attention. In verse 6 you will find Israel was greatly impoverished this word means pore or weak because of the Midianites and finally God got their attention and cried out to God, sometimes we have to go through destruction when we think we are tough and can do it on our own God is going to allow you to fill impoverished just like the Israelite.

7 And it came to pass, when the children of Israel cried unto the Lord because of the Midianites, 8 That the Lord sent a prophet unto the children of Israel, which

said unto them, Thus saith the Lord God of Israel, I brought you up from Egypt, and brought you forth out of the house of bondage; 9 And I delivered you out of the hand of the Egyptians, and out of the hand of all that oppressed you, and drove them out from before you, and gave you their land; 10 And I said unto you, I

am the Lord your God; fear not the gods of the Amorites, in whose land ye dwell: but ye have not obeyed my voice.

God delivered them out of pain and sorrow and the hand that oppressed Israel, God told them not to fear the gods of the land that was given to them but did not obey the Lord's voice. A prophet was sent to tell theme this now let us see what happens next...

11 And there came an angel of the Lord and sat under an oak which was in OPHAH, that pertained unto JOASH the Abiezrite: and his son Gideon threshed wheat by the winepress, to hide it from

the Midianites. 12 And the angel of the Lord appeared unto him, and said unto him, The Lord is with thee, thou mighty man of valor.

Okay so God Chose a man named Gideon who had no courage, who was scared, and the angel appeared to him and said in verse 12 and said The Lord is with thee, thou mighty man of valor. Valor means great courage in the face of danger, especially in battle. God sees past the weakness of our flesh he sees what we are capable of and not capable of and how dangerous we can be to fight back with courage.

So, God sent an angel to comfort him and tell him The Lord is with you, we often at times for getting the Lord is with us and we are mighty Valores fighting to get out of captivity, bondage. We are at war as of today we were at war the very moment the serpent tricked eave then eave convinced to eat this fruit.

To be honest, the very moment the devil decided to betray our Father in heaven it was war specifically because the Devil wanted God's throne what God gave to him was not enough selfish evil betrayal to our Father.

13 And Gideon said unto him, Oh my Lord, if the Lord be with us, why then is all this befallen us? and where be all his miracles which our fathers told us of, saying, Did not the Lord bring us up from Egypt? but now the Lord hath forsaken us and delivered us into the hands of the Midianites.

14 And the Lord looked upon him, and said, go in this thy might, and thou shalt save Israel from the hand of the Midianites: have not I sent thee?

15 And he said unto him, oh my Lord, wherewith shall I save Israel? behold, my family is poor in Manasseh, and I am the least in my father's house.

16 And the Lord said unto him, surely, I will be with thee, and thou shalt smite the Midianites as one man.

At first Gideon question, the angel of the Lord and the Lord told him well I'm here now and I chose you to go and fight but I will be with you in verse 16 says the Lord said unto him, Surely I will be with thee, and thou shalt smite the Midianites as one man. Meaning God is so powerful that when the Lord is with us no matter how many there is the Lord is there to defeat our enemies and to destroy them and to deliver them out of enemy's hand.

17 And he said unto him, if now I have found grace in thy sight, then shew me a sign that thou talk with me.

18 Depart not hence, I pray thee, until I come unto thee, and bring forth my present, and set it before thee. And he said I will tarry until thou come again.

19 And Gideon went in and made ready a kid, and unleavened cakes of an ephah of flour: the flesh he put in a basket, and he put the broth in a pot, and brought it out unto him under the oak, and presented it.

20 And the angel of God said unto him, Take the flesh and the unleavened cakes, and lay them upon this rock, and pour out the broth. And he did so.

21 Then the angel of the Lord put forth the end of the staff that was in his hand and touched the flesh and the unleavened cakes, and there rose up fire out of the rock and consumed the flesh and the unleavened cakes. Then the angel of the Lord departed out of his sight.

22 And when Gideon perceived that he was an angel of the Lord, Gideon said, Alas, O Lord God! for because I have seen an angel of the Lord face to face.

23 And the Lord said unto him, Peace is unto thee; fear not: thou shalt not die.

So Gideon wanted to bring a gift to the angel of the Lord to see if he was an angel from the Lord. Thinking from the back of his mind how can this be is this happening is this an angel from the Lord? So he asked the angel of the Lord to wait and he waited as he said he would bring forth his gift and did as the angel of the Lord said then he prayed to God I saw angel and the Lord said to Gideon in verse 23 Peace be unto thee; fear not: thou shalt not die. As long as the Lord said what he said to you and believe it shall be so. Remember God is the potter we are the clay when the potter speaks, he speaks to the power and promising over his people.

24 Then Gideon built an altar there unto the Lord, and called it Jehovah shalom: unto this day it is yet in OPHRAH of the Abiezrites.

25 And it came to pass the same night, that the Lord said unto him, Take thy father's young bullock, even the second bullock of seven years old, and throw down the altar of Baal that thy father hath, and cut down the grove that is by it:

26 And build an altar unto the Lord thy God upon the top of this rock, in the ordered place, and take the second bullock, and offer a burnt sacrifice with the wood of the grove which thou shalt cut down.

Chapter 5: Conquer Fear

27   Then Gideon took ten men of his
servants and did as the Lord had said
unto him: and it was so, because he
feared his father's household, and the
men of the city, that he could not do it by
day, that he did it by night.

Gideon built an altar and called it Jehovah
Shalom witch; means The Lord is peace.
Gideon found peace when he built the
altar and gave that peace back to God
and God told him gave him his first
instructions, started at the alter and
Gideon had to be very sneaky and careful
on how to handle this task at hand. There
are ways to sneak around the Devil and
not let him see your fear or plans to
destroy the works of the enemies. Gideon
cut down Baal that they worshiped to
leave a message War Has Just Be Gun.

28   And when the men of the city arose early in the morning, behold, the altar of Baal was cast down, and the grove was cut down that was by it, and the second bullock was offered upon the altar that was built.

29 And they said one to another, who hath done this thing? And when they enquired and asked, they said, Gideon the son of JOASH hath done this thing.

30 Then the men of the city said unto JOASH, bring out thy son, that he may die: because he hath cast down the altar of Baal, and because he hath cut down the grove that was by it.

31 And JOASH said unto all that stood against him, Will ye plead for Baal? will ye save him? he that will plead for him, let him be put to death whilst it is yet morning: if he is a god, let him plead for himself because one hath cast down his altar.

Remember in verse 23 the Lord told Gideon you will not die the enemies are already threatened at hand to have Gideon killed because he broke the law. Now don't get me wrong, the Lord said to obey the Laws of the land but God said not to worship any idols or any gods so this law is not good to the Lord even on earth.

They were all shocked who did this, who had the nerve to cast down Baal in verse 31 Joash said unto all that stood against him will ye plead for Baal? Will ye save him? He that will plead for him? Then they went on saying if Gideon is a god let him plead for himself because he cast down his altar. If he is a God; he will get himself out of this situation but you see they had no idea what they were up against. When the Devil does not know your plans on how to conquer your battles or to get out of slavery, out of bondage, out of captivity but he knows you got to be up to something then he starts consuming in fear on how to try to demolish your plans threw the Lord But don't ever give upturn your ears from your enemies and turn your ears tore the heavens but that is who is your God, your Father, Your potter for he is the potters hand who created you and this world and you in it. Rise above your fear and be valor, just like Gideon.

32 Therefore on that day, he called him Jerubbaal, saying, Let Baal plead against him because he hath thrown down his altar.

33 Then all the Midianites and the Amalekites and the children of the east were gathered together, and went over, and pitched in the valley of Jezreel. 34 But the Spirit of the Lord came upon Gideon, and he blew a trumpet, and Abiezer was gathered after him.

35 And he sent messengers throughout all Manasseh; who also was gathered after him: and he sent messengers unto Asher, and Zebulun, and unto Naphtali; and they came up to meet them.

36 And Gideon said unto God, If thou wilt save Israel by mine hand, as thou hast said,

 37 Behold, I will put a fleece of wool in the floor; and if the dew be on the fleece only, and it be dry upon all the earth beside, then shall I know that thou wilt save Israel by mine hand, as thou hast said. Uh-oh, here we go it is getting intense now.

Okay so Gideon spoke out of faith if you say I am the one to deliver your people out this is awesome in verse 36 Gideon said unto God, If thou wilt save Israel by mine hand, as thou hast said verse 37 This is Gideon speaking with power fleece of wool in the floor, dew be on the fleece only testing God to see if God was still there by his side I believe that with all my heart Gideon new that a war is being put in place he wanted to make sure before he stepped foot in the battleground before he went to battle. This is how we need to be we need to make sure where we are with the Lord before we step into battle Gideon prepared himself self and we need to prepare our self's in battle as well. Not only did he prepare himself he was also afraid

38 And it was so: for he rose up early on the morrow, and thrust the fleece together, and wrung the dew out of the fleece, a bowl full of water.

39 And Gideon said unto God, Let not thine anger be hot against me, and I will speak but this once: let me prove, I pray thee, but this once with the fleece; let it now be dry only upon the fleece, and upon all the ground let there be dew.

40 And God did so that night: for it was dry upon the fleece only, and there was dew on all the ground.

Father God I ask you right now in the name of Jesus Christ whoever may read this by their eyes they shall receive a bondage or a slave of an act in their life to rise above their fear to defeat it by the grace of your power to free them from there snare as you have done for Gideon or even for the Israelite's to rise above every fear they have ever come against or even faced in their life Lord comfort them as you did Gideon and change their life forever. Amen...

Chapter 6: What Your Made Of

Hebrews 4:12 For the word of God is quick and powerful and sharper than any two-edged sword piercing even to the dividing asunder of soul and spirit and the joints and marrow and is a discerner of the thoughts and intents of the heart. awaken the Holy Spirit that is planted within you remember your made from the potter's hands you have his DNA all your missing is your faith. Fight, Fight, Fight through the word of God and sometimes if you just be still God will do it for you depending on the situation and your relationship with the Lord.

If you are a broken vessel like I was God can deliver you from it.

He can mold you and make you whole again and what is scared are the most beautiful scars so make it shine like no other and the word of God tells us No weapon that is formed against will Not Prosper. I did some research on Asunder and what it means, Asunder means: into separate parts; in or into pieces: Lightning split the old oak tree asunder.

apart or widely separated: as wide asunder as the polar regions.

Now I want to talk to you about David. He was just a little a boy teenager when he defeated the Goliath. He found his faith as his passion in his heart in God. It is a challenge to put passion in your heart but what helps through that is to put passion in your heart to win, win and fight like you never fought before.

Growth in the Spirit of a battle:

Now what got my attention was how tall Goliath was in a human form of 9 feet and 3 meters, now look at David see he was just a little boy they said. But God never looked at David's high, he looks at his bravery, his faith, his spiritual life, his obedience. Now David told Goliath you come with armor a shield a sword, but look at what I came with.

But cents you mentioned yourself as a dog of questioning yourself after I get done with you; I'm going to feed you to the animals. So now look who is going to devour you once I cut your he'd off.

An enemy will question his self of what they are and call them own self in question. I courage you to read 1st Samuel 17:43-47 on your own. You see this is the kind of faith David had once my God delivers you which is an enemy into my hand's I'm going to take you down with my sling shot now remember he got 5 smooth stones and only used one. Now when spoke in versus 45through 47 the Lord showed me something, speaking not only in Confidence, speaking not only from the strength of his courage, but all in faith. Is there confidence and courage in your faith? How tall are you spiritually?

God put a question on my heart are you getting tired of yourself who has fear and you run because you see a spirit of Goliath that you have to face? I don't know about you but theme Israelites were pretty scared running in fright and fear. Then David comes along, first, he defeated bear than a lion. Do you know how David was big and tall on the inside? Or how he got that way spiritually? A Spiritual Tall Man. Those who looked after the flack wasn't always week. That was David's job. He would always pray in confidence by believing in God, believing in yourself... Why not, this is theory in my heart that he knew God believed in him. Especially if God stripped the anointing from Saul and found favor a pone David to anointed as King. But it took a process a battle to learn even more about trusting God as a king.

Chapter 7: Your Battle Belongs Too Thee Lord

1 Samuel 17:48-51

Remember David's last words before he ran after Goliath with his slingshot at the end of verse 47 for the battle is the Lords, and he will give you into my hands I just want you to see how David puts God before him in Battle. The Lord said someone needs to be reminded how God was with David the entire time when he faced Goliath now listen to this, Now when Goliath drew to get ready to meet David I think Goliath felt God's power and began to be afraid because verse 48 says he got ready David was already ready he took off probably with a sprint be so cool to see that dirt thrashing in dust behind him by the power of God.

In Ch 49-50 David got out a stone and used his slingshot now listen to this he swung that rock so, so, so, so hard that stone sunk into Goliath's head. David had no armor any sword on him he went and got his enemies sword Goliath's sword and cut off his head in verse 51 and continuing in verse 51 saying When the philistines saw that their champion was dead, they fled.

If you can find the whole root of your battle the strongest enemies in the battle you have to face use your spiritual stone and then use the enemies sword to cut off its head those demons don't want to fight anymore because there champion is dead so they fled I don't want to be a part of this anymore we are week without our champ let's get out of here.

Learn how to build your confidence and courage through your faith and destroy your enemies. 1st Samuel 17:52-58 okay so Now David is getting ready to go fight the philistine and put Galieth's armor in the tent, now he carried the head and left the armor, the entire time till they got done destroying their enemies.

David was brought to the king and still carrying the head of Goliath, He showed evidence the enemy is dead by carrying the head and this is my theory why he carried the head when he could have left it in the tent. He carried the head to show the people not to be afraid the worst is over God is with us David saw and believed these were the chosen soldier by the Lord and by carrying the head to show it is okay have faith courage be strong in the Lord for you are the Lord's army. Now I'm going to throw a curveball and step into The Armor of God:

- With confidence, you are strengthening your armor

- With courage, you are strengthening a strong barrier of armor

- With Faith, your strengthening your shield which is a shield of faith

- With the Word of God; you are sharpening your sword or even hey your slingshot

- With Truth, you are strengthening your helmet to prevent the flaws or the lies of the Devil

- With your Feet that is planted with his feet strengthens the Shoes on your feet.

Chapter 8: Devil Wants What Was Made Fore You

Devil don't get anything on you, he can't break through the barrier of your armor, Devil is a thief he wants what you have but he can't have it keep fighting to keep winning

Let us be like David he knew the enemy mocked God's army, we are God's army fight, fight, fight. This is what I believe, Yes God will test your faithfulness, but he will also test what is a week and what is strong. What is already strong will be stronger, I prayed and asked the Lord I said Lord I feel lopsided, What, is week, is week, What, is strong, is strong. I feel lopsided, I want what is week, to be strong.

So the Lord will test of how week it is to see what kind of battle to put you in to strengthen your weakness now, of course, the Devil will all ways try to take a peek or poke at you and send someone to slow you down or even pop a tire spiritually but that is what strengthens you replacing what is week because it ware and tare, on you.

Now, remember my prayer I prayed, the next day I begin to fill week, shaky tired, a little dizzy... My sugar dropped so the battle begins, my mind playing tricks on me anger surrounding me, no energy...

Ephesians CH 6 came to my mind the whole armor of God so I go in my back yard for some air and I begin to just lift my hands and pray the Holy Spirit came over me and said this, The Devil Don't Have Nothing On You, He can't break through the barrier of the armor of God that is upon you, He wants what you have He can't have it! When you go through battle devil is not going to follow the rules, he will try to rip you apart he tries to tare' down what is strong to be the week. The word of God says no Demon

Nor angels nor man can separate my love from my GOD!!!

John9:4 I must work the works of him that sent me, while it is day: the night cometh when no man can work. God always has a backup plan when you need help with the mission God sent you on listening to this, call upon the name of the Lord and he will send a night, the night cometh when no man can work.

Talk about a rescue team on its way and some of you need a rescue team to pull you out of fear or even fight off the Demons you lost control of the fight from the beginning.

Chapter 9: The Power of Asunder

And this is what polar regions are: The polar regions, also called the frigid zones, of Earth, are the regions of the planet that surround its geographical poles (the North and South Poles), lying within the polar circles.

So, with that said this is what the Holy Spirit showed me picture a globe which is world map and picture that right in front of you now.

Take that old oak tree and put it at the top of the world and watch the lightning strike it in half now its split its separating and meeting all the way from left to right of the opposite direction from each other now watch it meat up with each other in your mind it's going to explode when it, meats together on the other side of the world and evaporate be no more.

That is what God does to our enemies if we allow him too. Pretty cool huh... This is what it means going into battle but not alone, fight as David fought and the ones like king Saul who disobeyed God, he stripped the anointing off of him and anointed David to be King. Because of obedience.

Let us obey the Lord and listen to his voice he will guide you. The Holy Spirit is not just a weapon but also a gift as well and to lead us to the fountain where we will never thirst again.

Fighting to your way out of slavery or bondage is not easy, for it is very hard and time-consuming specifically because you have to fight your way through all the memory good or bad or even the worst to find that switch and turn it off leave it off and never look back be what God called you to be: Asunder and fight a good fight.

Being captives in our minds can also be dangerous because of dangerous thoughts, such as suicidal, not worth anything, can't ever amount to anything. It's a lie Don't kill yourself, don't waste your life away. God has a higher purpose for us he has a higher calling in our lives; 2 Chronicles 7:14 If my people, which are called by my name, shall humble themselves, and pray, and seek my face, and turn from their wicked ways; then will I hear from heaven, and will forgive their sin, and will heal their land.

Chapter 10: God Has A Gift for You Inn Battle

Figure out what your gifts are and use them to help yourself get stronger and fight your way out of your battle one of my gifts is writing poetry:

(Lesson Learned)

The fillings that run in my heart like a rushing wave in my blood, overlapping a feeling with fear that turns into courage. Lesson learned... The fillings that burst like a flood of persuasion and multiple fireballs times a thousand to destroy my whole atmosphere of the roots of my baring soul... Fight, fight, fight... Lesson learned... The gage of a roaring lion who dwells in your presents while you chase for something you lack from the baring of the tips of your toes, as you begin to hear a voice in your ear of the lesson of wisdom, patient's, faith…. Lesson learned. The soft presents of a lamb, for its blood, is pure and holy, for its cote of fur blemishes its warmth of security and protection. For Jesus is the lamb who was slain and his blood was shed for me. Lesson Learned...

(What Do You Have for Me Too Day My Lord) What do you have for me today my Lord?

Are you going to break me down one last time?

Are you going to send down another bucket of your anointing power?

What do you have for me today my Lord?

Are you going to pore in me one last time like a roaring thunderstorm and flood the atmosphere once more?

Is there one last set of your crushing for the purest of pure of your oil to run in my veins and bones once more?

What do you have for me today my Lord?

Perhaps one more touch one more powerful touch from grace to grace from your holly of holly's, to take me past the altar into your holiness. Yes, yes, this is what I pray my Lord a one more last night of your revival one more powerful move of you from grace to grace to take me past the alters into your holly place

Amen.

I Courage you, if you can beat it, you can defeat it, if you can defeat it, then you can be delivered from it.

Chapter 11: The Recovery Room

Introduced: A Testimony

A living walking healing transformed, conqueror, deliverer advocate healer, for giver

Philippian's 2:6-7

• 6 Who in the form of God, thought it not robbery to be equal with God:

• 7 But made himself of no reputation, and took upon him the form of a servant, and was made in the likeness of men:

Deliver:

The whole purpose of him coming in a likeness of a man in a humbled and humility way with the package of agape love know no man could ever understand the capacity of his love and risen from the grave with the holy spirit and taught his disciples that power delivers saves and He came, He lived, and he died. He delivered his message to the sinners.

Healer:

He healed the blind, the lame to walk, the disease hilled, the broken hearted that was crushed from there iniquities, set the captive free that was captivated by their flesh.

Jesus conquered the grave, if Jesus is walking through the grave, I am walking to, no grave going hold my body down.

For-giver:

- Even though he was persecuted, betrayed, disappointed, mocked, denied.

- Some of us at times for get that Jesus knows what it feels like to be betrayed when we are betrayed, a beaten not like his beating his beating was so that the ripping of his flesh and horrifying pain and blood shed for the world. Or maybe some of us has been betrayed. People disappointed you, mocked you, or even denied you.

- Jesus came as a baby, grew as a flesh, walked as a man died as a king, and all for what to teach you to forgive and let go.

The whole purpose of Jesus creating a testimony that God create is not just for the cross but for you too. To testify of the living inside of you that you have in you. Reborn and the old has died so there for you are walking as a reborn of the child of God, a walking testimony.

Way-maker:

- Jesus took his disciples in a storm for a reason, to build them up, when there seems to be no way not all hope is lost but yet our flesh seems to give in so easily. Its week, Jesus told his disciples before he sweated blood from his brow, your flesh is weak o but your spirit is willing.

- Faith turns into possible, possible turns in to making a way when there seems to be no way, through man all things are impossible, but through God all things are possible.

When we go through storms people often wonder why does this happen to us, it's not the fact that it happened to you, you are going through a storm to get you to the other side to make you stronger to build you up. Jesus told his disciples your flesh is weak but yet your spirit is willing.

Mountain-mover:

• Not by might, nor by power but by my spirit, says the Lord of hosts.

• A true gospel believer moves mountains, how is that? Prayer turning yourself into a prayer warrior and God hearing his soldier's pray and seek after him by his spirit that mountain shall be moved.

• Knowing, and believing are different. Just because you know it, does not mean you will believe it. God wants you to know him, He also wants you to believe in him. Exceedingly, abundantly, and above all.

If you are to pray, and to fast those mountains to be moved, those mountains have to obey you because you are speaking with faith, you are working on it. When you fast, you are eating the word of God, when you read the word of God this is your meal your spiritual meal and

when you pray, you are receiving
strength. For the ones who do you wrong
God will make all things right. He will
make it right for you.

Conqueror:

Definition-

One who conqueror, one who gains a
victory, one who subdues and brings into
subjection or possession, by force or by
influence. The man who defeats his
antagonist in combat is a conqueror, as
the generoral, or admiral who defeat's his
enemies.

Note:

A plan that was brought out so perfectly,
you see the Devil thought he could make
a fool out of God and that Jesus was a big
disappointment to him. But that wasn't
the case though was it, a distraction of
Jesus body left in the tomb and those

who loved him dearly wept not knowing a pain for distraction, the key was robed, the grave was robed, the door was opened the Conqueror brings possession by influence of a strategic death.

God all ways has a perfect plan our plans are worthless. When we try to do it our self's it never seems to work out the way we want it to because God knows better.

Runner:

- Running after Jesus, because he ran after us to save us from eternal damnation. From our own self, from the Devil, from being tormented in hell. A powerful runner will pray, a powerful runner will exercise their spiritual relationship with the Lord.

- I want to point something out to you. The women that suffered 12 years of bleeding. She chased after healing spent all that she had to do whatever it took, she heard Jesus was in town. One last run one more time, but you see her last race she had to fight through a crowed to get her healing for her race was not a finish line, for her race was: if I could just touch the helm of his garment.

- O but a man was already on a run for his daughter to be healed, somebody touched me, come on let's go she's dying.

- A parent will run for their child to be healed, saved, sanctified filled with the holy Ghost.

- She is only asleep, then all of the sudden all of the unbelievers were demanded to get out.

There are 2 different runners, A runner running after sin, and a runner running after God. A true believer runner will run for their hilling, God will push all the un believers out of your way just keep running that race never give up run that race with faith and mountains will be moved out of your way.

CH 12 The Change "In" Me

Changer: Isaiah 64:8, Psalms 51:10

- 8 And yet, O Lord you are our Father. We are the clay and you are the potter. We all are formed by your hand.

- 10 Create in me a clean heart, O God: and renew a right spirit within me.

- A broken heart, can be renewed but the scars remain. A broken spirit, can be renewed God is the potter the master of art of creating his people formed by his hands

- Change cannot begin until you step out into the potter's hands. There is one condition in this process is this: TRUST

IN HIM THROUGH THE CHANGE (THE RENEWING)

- When God brought me out of the captivity that I was in, my spirit was broken, my soul was so tired, my body was so beat up from he'd to my toes, I had bruises on my feet. I felt that I had no more fight left in me....

When I left Oklahoma to my parents I had to go through a rough battle of deliverance I was influenced into some hard drugs in my life I was addicted to heavy drugs the lord called upon me I kept you alive for a reason so there for you are going to go through my deliverance.

I did not go to rehab or nothing. I have Godly parents who stood by my side who comforted me through this hard captivity because that is what drugs do to you it's nothing but captivity putting you through this lie of illness I need it I need it it's the only thing that helps me...

 no it's a lie it will not help you, it will destroy you, drugs can kill you and that is what the Devil want's he wants no resurrection in our life's no victory what so ever...

My dad would talk with me my daughter you cannot keep yourself down like this you have to find the strength to get up because God strength is there and you have children you have to be strong for them, get up dust yourself off.

It hurts as long as it does for reason to keep you from going back it is a reminder to you so you don't go back, When you hurt and God put's you where you are stay there Bond with your father at the beginning of your pain.

When a battle knocks you down, while you are there pray, then get back up and dust yourself off and move forward.

Don't stay down get up dust yourself off
God has plans for you work for you to be
done, O' and when you do get up you will
be surprised of how tall you are
spiritually.

We have got to have confidence in our
own self and belief. We are to destroy
our enemies before the enemies destroys
us.

Women Pray before you go to bed why?
Because you are a threat to the devil
when you wake up.

A powerful testimony to Waken
somebody's heart. Jesus walked beside us
as a flesh he will walk be side us
spiritually he promised he will never leave
you nor will he ever forsake you.

CH 13 Holy Ghost "Interring In"

Holy spirit-filler: Acts 2:4, Acts 4:31, Mark 16:18

- 4 And every one present was filled with the Holy Spirt and began speaking in other languages, as the Holy Spirit gave them this ability.

- 31 After this prayer, the meeting place shook, and they were filled with the Holy Spirit. Then they preached the word of God with boldness.

- 18 They shall take up serpents; and if they drink any deadly thing, it shall not hurt them; they shall lay hands on the sick, and they shall recover.

- After I received the holy spirit, I started learning how to fight my battles. When you ask Jesus in to your heart it doesn't stop there you go on a journey and see what else God has for you.

- Jesus told his disciples that he had given them the permission and the power to preach the gospel during this time they were being trained be for he died on the cross and be for acts.

- Holy spirit will help you, lead you, guide you, fight against temptation. But it won't do that unless you are praying in spirit of the Lord.

- For some, temptation is not just based on drugs, but on their flesh.

- What are you saying? Thinking with your flesh instead of thinking with your spirit. If you have an intimate relationship with the Lord in your heart and your Spirit, it takes discipline. I am talking about encourage yourself and to pray without ceasing.

When I first Got the Holy ghost

After I received the Holy Spirit, most people feel that wow not me, that pain was still there, if I shouted, I shouted in pain, every chance I took I felt as if what God has hurry up before its gone, yeah okay great Idea, no not great Idea.

God told me what are you doing, I'm right here there is plenty to go around God told me I will never run out where does it say in the word that I will run out, my fountain will always overflow.

After 8 months passed, I started noticing progress in my life, I started to fill stronger and see the strength in me through the Lord, Word of Wisdom, Word of Knowledge, taking me places in my life spiritually that I have never experienced before.

LEADING-GUIDING

I don't know how many times I felt a hand grab me and no one was there, I don't know how many times I felt the Lord hold me and no one was there, I don't know how many times I heard a whisper in my ear and no one was there.

STEPPING OUT OF YOUR COMFORT ZONE

• Did you know that you can help someone to have mountains moved?

• That question was also whispered into my ear

• Bond with your father at the beginning of your pain, you cannot do it yourself or you will suffer, if you bond with your father you will begin to connect with the Lord.

Ch 14 Let Go, Let God

Mathew 17:20-21 20

So Jesus said to them, "Because of your unbelief; for assuredly, I say to you, if you have faith as a mustard seed, you will say to this mountain, 'Move from here to there,' and it will move; and nothing will be impossible for you. 21 However, this kind does not go out except by prayer and fasting."

Mark 11:22-26

22 And Jesus answering saith unto them, Have faith in God.

23 For verily I say unto you, That whosoever shall say unto this mountain, Be thou removed, and be thou cast into the sea; and shall not doubt in his heart, but shall believe that those things which

he saith shall come to pass; he shall have whatsoever he saith.

24 Therefore, I say unto you, what things so ever ye desire, when ye pray, believe that ye receive them, and ye shall have them.

25 And when ye stand praying, forgive, if ye have ought; against any: that your Father also which is in heaven may forgive you your trespasses.

26 But if ye do not forgive, neither will your Father which is in heaven forgive your trespasses.

- God is about to take you for a ride of your life.

- What you got loose to give up all the bad to gain what is better for you?

- It is not worth holding on to all the bad. But it is worth giving up the pain because God wants us happy and not in bondage of pain or the price of the pain.

That is a lie straight of the pits of hell Jesus already paid the price for you he did his part so now it is our turn to be submissive unto the Lord.

If you do not ask the Lord to forgive you of your sins and you have "hate" in your heart God will not forgive you it starts with you first you have to forgive yourself first before you can for your neighbor. The purpose of Jesus Lord walked this earth to introduce his love, Lord walked this earth to hill his people as a message and to train his disciples to get the world ready for his coming, Lord walked this earth to partake of communion with his disciples: The bred represents the body that was broken, the wine that represents his blood the cleansing, Lord walked this earth to take the punishment on the cross for you that what so ever is in your life to be crucified, when its crucified it is on the cross. When you let it go and you surrender yourself unto the cross it is crucified leave it there.

CH 15 Your Done When God Says You Are Done

You are not done yet

Acts 5:18-24

Acts 5:18-24 New American Bible 18   19 laid hands upon the apostles and put them in the public jail. But during the night, the angel of the Lord opened the doors of the prison, led them out, and said, 20 "Go and take your place in the temple area, and tell the people everything about this life." 21

When they heard this, they went to the temple early in the morning and taught. When the high priest and his companions arrived, they convened the Sanhedrin, the full senate of the Israelites, and sent to the jail to have them brought in. 22 But the court officers who went did not find them in the prison, so they came back and reported, 23 "We found the jail securely locked and the guards stationed outside the doors, but when we opened them, we found no one inside." 24 When they heard this report, the captain of the temple guard and the chief priests were at a loss about them, as to what this would come to.

If I was in charge in a position that he was in I would be scared in fear, not one time did he mention how did you get out not one time he was afraid.

I don't know about you but I'm not done tarring down walls of the devil, I'm not done spreading revival not just in my life but in others. I'm not done working and building for the kingdom of God, I'm not done marching for the Lord, I'm not done shouting out In The Name OF Jesus Christ for every demand in hell shall tremble when they hear his name that their own fear blows up their own territory from shaking so much.

Start walking and Living your victorious testimony. A testimony God brought you out of and testimony of Jesus dying on the cross, God's testimony to be alive in you His supplication, His love, His deliverance, He is a savior he saved you from death and allowed life to be everlasting never ending. God's Testimony "Of" His Son Jesus Christ.

After I had learned I was ten feet tall in the Lord I asked how tall was goliath, 9 feet tall, I said I am taller than he is. You must have confidence in yourself to be able to carry faith that moves mountains.

The next battle that I was going through feeling alone wanting someone to be right there by my side so I started looking for a friend on a dating sight. On CDFF sight that is Christian Dating Fore Free sight. All I wanted was a friend but the way I was looking for a friend because I felt alone was wrong, the wrong way. The

Lord gave me a dream to fight against what I was feeling because I am not alone. We all walk through storms but if we have our Lord Jesus Christ with in us and us opened up to him, he can provide every need, every miraculous need in our life's. David said in Psalms Though I walk through the valley of the shadow of death, I shall fear no evil for you are with me, your rod and your staff they comfort me. We will go through some kind of battle but know this we are not alone for the rod and the staff they comfort us. If we allow the word of God to comfort us God shows up with so much of comfort.

CH 16 The Devil Will Test Your Faith

When I first started preaching and learning how to fight against the whiles of the devil I was being tested. Me and both my daughters had to sleep in the same bed during this time, late at night I woke up about 2:30 am and I saw this thick like burnt shaggy hair at first I thought it was my mom's dog, the thickness of the filling in the air got so thick with fear and that demonic feeling, wait a minute my door was shut, it is cracked open, okay, I sit up and I hear this heavy breathing on the corner of my bed, I could not see nothing, I lay back down, ten minutes later, I see my first daughter her legs was lifted up in the air and was pulled to the edge of the bed, then my second daughter's legs was lifted up and pulled to the edge of the bed, I grab them both and I feel a tug on both of them pulling on them and I said out loud Devil I dare you to tress pass and to touch my children I call upon God and said this: Lord I don't know what is going on but no body touches my kids and you promised me that no one or nothing will hurt me and my family again, there legs drop then I said demon you are tress passing and because I called upon the Lord my angel will beat you to the pulp for touching my kids I rebuke you In the Name Of Jesus Christ, I could hear wrestling and in the hall way it was as if I could hear something being dragged. God will always protect his children. But you have to call upon the Lord.

Day and night going through the battle of filling alone but one thing that helped me was when I would read the word and pray, I felt as if I was not alone, I felt the presents of Jesus there with me. The word tells us he walked as a man by our side, he walks with us in the spirit of the Lord and he also prays for us he intercedes for the world daily. We are not alone all it takes is prayer time with Jesus he loves us so much that he died for us for our sins because hell was not made for you and I, there is more Jesus is wanting to share his kingdom with us. Having anxiety can cause you to fill so much emotion and make you fill like you are on a roller coaster constantly feeling anxious, it will put you through a spiritual battle that you will not win on your own, we cannot fight battles by our self's... We have got to find the soldier within us and strengthen it through the word of the sword and through fasting and praying. The word of God tells us to pray without ceasing.

1 Thessalonians 5:16-28 King James Version (KJV) 16

Rejoice evermore. 17

Pray without ceasing. 18

In everything give thanks: for this is the will of God in Christ Jesus concerning you. 19

Quench not the Spirit. 20

Despise not prophesying's. 21

Prove all things; hold fast that which is good. 22

Abstain from all appearance of evil. 23

And the very God of peace sanctify you wholly; and I pray God your whole spirit and soul and body be preserved blameless unto the coming of our Lord Jesus Christ. 24

Faithful is he that calleth you, who also will do it. 25

Brethren, pray for us. 26

Greet all the brethren with a holy kiss. 27

I charge you by the Lord that this epistle be read unto all the holy brethren. 28

The grace of our Lord Jesus Christ be with you. Amen.

We struggle with this because we do not pray enough or read the word enough or believe enough or lift each other up enough or carry the Love we are suppose, to have in our hearts. Yes, we struggle, we get upset, the word tells us to be upset with sin BUT it is the action of the approach we make to choose the madness that we allow to acer in our own actions. Why did you choose the word madness? I am glad you asked madness can cause an invite of anger to stay and when it stays it will corrupt and cause darkness from the inside. Such rage of anger of wanting revenge constantly and not letting go of the past. The word of God tells us we can be angry but sin not:

Ephesians 4:26 King James Version (KJV) 26 Be ye angry, and sin not: let not the sun go down upon your wrath:

What Paul says is, "Be angry but do not sin; do not let the sun go down on your anger, and do not make room for the devil." What he is saying here is that we can get angry. Anger is a natural human emotion and not a bad one in and of itself. Yes when we are angry we are going to be in pain, it hurts to be angry but don't let that pain over power you or overcome you and cause you to be the victim when God made us to be stronger than that to be victorious, overcomer to overcome our battles to move mountains to run a race and to never stop to grip on and to never let go.

CH 17 Let Go What Does Not Belong Too You

The word says Let not your heart be troubled:

John 14:1-3 King James Version (KJV)

14 Let not your heart be troubled: ye believe in God, believe also in me. 2

In my Father's house are many mansions: if it were not so, I would have told you. I go to prepare a place for you. 3

And if I go and prepare a place for you, I will come again, and receive you unto myself; that where I am, there ye may be also.

Give up your troubles to the Lord for there is a promise that he is coming back soon and very soon we will see the king. We will never know the time or the hour. All of us suffer from some kind of trouble such as anxiety, depression, fear, DPSD there is all sorts of trouble that all of us need to focus on letting go just do it don't ponder on it any longer just do it just let it go and receive your victory in Jesus.

As I am going through this journey of God equipping me, I have learned along the way joy is our strength, joy does not all ways mean being happy. Now laughter is healing to the heart, it's medicine:

Proverbs 17:22 King James Version (KJV) 22

A merry heart doeth good like a medicine: but a broken spirit drieth the bones.

Allow yourself to be merry, Cheerfulness of spirit has a great influence upon the body, and much contributes to the health and welfare of it. Jesus wants us strong healthy and happy. Let's not allow our spirits to be broken we don't want our bones to be dried up because whatever comes your way will shatter you every single time the more you allow yourself to be broken from a dried, up bone will cause you to want to die. The eight months I went through I had a broken spirit and whatever came at me when a part of me broke because I was so week all of me broke and I just wanted to die I did not want to live, when you are broken it is not easy to overcome, it is scary, emotional sting that never stops, a pounding of a sore that you just want to rip off because you know it doesn't belong there. Over time of fighting and not giving you feel the difference when you keep fighting. Fight a good fight and don't give in:

2 Timothy 4:7-8 King James Version (KJV) 7

I have fought a good fight, I have finished my course, I have kept the faith: 8

Henceforth there is laid up for me a crown of righteousness, which the Lord, the righteous judge, shall give me at that day:

and not to me only, but unto all them also that love his appearing.

If you give up your fight, you give up your crown, and if you give up your crown you give up your name that is written in the lambs book of life, and if you give up your name then you are not saved and you do not love Jesus.

Those who love Jesus will be faithful with faith and love and fight a good fight and never give up their crown.

The only decision that should be made of when you give up your crown is when you are at the feet of Jesus and you toss your crown to his feet because he deserves it.

Jesus payed a debt that I owed that the world owed for there is mercy in Jesus there is Love, Joy, Strength for strength comes from the lord and Joy comes in the morning.

When you decide to wake up one day and know that you are happy, there is a saying if you keep smiling like that it's going to get stuck, allow it to get stuck in your heart never "loose" that smile, the smile that you have is yours you fought for it, so do not abuse this smile because you can abuse a smile, you can abuse your own heart.

By living in sin is selfish so there for you are abusing your own self. Don't do that to yourself God want's us happy healthy and strong in the Lord.

Ch 18 Build, Build, Build High Go Higher

Learn how to build yourself up and learn how to except some one of helping you build yourself up, because if you don't you will take everything the wrong way. We all need to be encouraged, to be lifted up by our brothers and sisters in Christ and to pray for one another. Always pray for one another. Always lift each other up. Always pray for those who do you wrong because God will make it right. Always pray for those who are there for you because they need you too and God will give them strength to. All these prayers will come together and make you strong. Prayer Releases Power.

From Thee Distance

The hardest thing to learn how to do is to swim through all your memories, weather it is happy memories or bad memories that happened to you. This is what I went through every single day, I didn't want to I felt as if I was not strong enough for anything in my life any more. I had to do this for me so that I would learn how to forgive for me. The hardest thing to learn how to do is to forgive yourself first especially if you put your kids in any situation you have to forgive yourself through everything just so you can gain courage to forgive your enemy your neighbors your loved one that you trusted that hurt you the most your best friend that you thought you could trust so deeply and broke that trust, your spouse or use to be your spouse pray for the ones who hurt you. Why, why would I do that after what they did to me? Because if you hold on to it your holding on to death its self. What do you mean? The word of God says hatred causes death we have to forgive for we do not know what they do, Jesus said on the cross before he released his spirit to God's hands he said Father forgive them for they do not know what they do, also in scripture says:

Mark 11:25-26

25

And when ye stand praying, forgive, if ye have "ought" against any: that your Father also which is in heaven may forgive you your trespasses. 26

But if ye do not forgive, neither will your Father which is in heaven forgive your trespasses.

Psalms 66:18

If I hold on to iniquity in my heart, the Lord will not hear me:

I do not recommend any one to have hatred in your hearts, it is more painful to hold on to then to let it go. I would rather hold peace in my heart then hold unforgiveness and wondering if God heard my prayers or not. How do I know I have forgiveness in my heart? You say a prayer as frequently as you do when you pray you pray this, Lord I have hurt in side of my heart and I don't know how to forgive please teach me to forgive so I do not hinder my relationship with you, I have so much hurt from the past and I don't know how to let it go show me how to lay it down. Keep praying that prayer and eventually you will start filling noticing and seeing the difference in side of your heart. When God was walking me through this and I was separated from my husband I had to learn how to love him from the distance because I prayed a prayer Lord I do not want to divorce him while I am angry teach me how to do this in "away" that it will impact my life and my children's life as well. It is not easy to learn how to love and forgive from the distance. I had to learn how to Respect my self, love myself, most importantly Forgive myself. These 3 important things to learn how to do when you come out of a domestic abuse relationship is not easy, you fill murdered on the inside and you literally fill dead, useless worthless. Vengeance belongs to the Lord we are to give up our anger and wrath for God says what wrath and punishment is given out he knows better than we do in scripture says:

Romans 12:19 King James Version (KJV) 19

Dearly beloved, avenge not yourselves, but rather give "place" unto wrath: for it is written, Vengeance is mine; I will repay, saith the Lord.

Deuteronomy 32:35

35 It is mine to avenge; I will repay. In due time their foot will slip; their day of disaster is near and their doom rushes upon them."

Romans 12:18

18 If it is possible, as far as it depends on you, live at peace with everyone.

Ch 19 Obtaining Knowledge "And" Strength Every Day

After 8 months of going through my recovery and through deliverance from drugs and relearning how to eat on a daily basis and in the middle of it all discovering strength along the way, when God gives you "strength" he gives you power to along with that strength.

Psalm 46:1-3 God is our refuge and strength, an ever-present help in trouble...

Proverbs 18:10 The name of the Lord is a strong tower; the righteous run into it and are safe. Nehemiah 8:10 Do not grieve, for the joy of the Lord is your strength.

The more I read the word the more I prayed the stronger I felt the safer I felt because the Lord put me in his strong tower.

Being in his strong tower is like being in the recovery room because while I was there the Lord renewed all of me, my strength, my mind, my heart, my life a healing process that takes time to hill from the roots.

Do not leave that tower until you are healed, do not leave that tower until God equips you to be prepared for another battle, do not leave that tower until God says you are ready to leave the tower.

Never rush your healing allow yourself to learn from your mistake and not regret the past learn from it and move forward, what is done is done, it cannot be undone. You Can Not Change "Thee" Past.

Leave the past in the past. Move forward for what is a head focus on what is in front of you and let go of what was except for what is and let God, that means let go of your past except what is present right now and let God do his job of what happened in the past and allow God to make everything right again.

Going even further in the process of perjured equipping you in silver and getting you ready for Gold to be purified and go through the fire to purify and shape you while you are hot.

It is a lot harder to shape you while your sword is cold, It is better to be hot to shape it nice and straight after the shaping got to go through the trial of sharpening to strengthen yourself the sword with in your heart what this is, is sharpening the asunder with in you the word of God is your asunder your sword for Hebrews 4:12 once again God is sharper than any two edged sword. But God has to shape you into that powerful weapon that God called you to be so that you can defeat your trials. Every newborn Christian has a calling on thier hearts God has a place for you he has a plan for you.

Zechariah 13:9 - And I will bring the third part through the fire, and will refine them as silver is refined, and will try them as gold is tried: they shall call on my name, and I will hear them: I will say, It [is] my people: and they shall say, The LORD [is] my God.

1 Peter 1:7 - That the trial of your faith, being much more precious than of gold that perisheth, though it be tried with fire, might be found unto praise and honour and glory at the appearing of Jesus Christ:

1 Peter 5:10 - But the God of all grace, who hath called us unto his eternal glory by Christ Jesus, after that ye have suffered a while, make you perfect, stablish, strengthen, settle [you].

Ch 20 A Spiritual Physical Battle

January 1st-2020 Before this date I was still going through a divorce, God told me during my trial two years before this date your husband will pass away, he will not make it much longer nothing you can do to change my mind. Plead for mercy for God to change his mind. The Lord Gave a me a scripture:

Do not touch my chosen people, "Do" not do my prophets no harm 1 Chronicles 16:22 NLT.

I lost my husband through death it was so hard on me on January-26-2020 that was on a Sunday I woke up feeling so funny in my face not knowing what in the world is going on and I did not feel good that day at all but I pushed on.

After me and my family got to the church I started to fill worse my face was going num I asked my dad to pray for me lay hands on me, dad pray for me right now dad I don't feel so good dad something is so wrong wright now pray for me.

I felt so heavy not knowing what I am up against that can be very scary fighting what you do not know what you are up against this trial was to teach me to give it to God immediately so I did.

After I got prayed for I decided to believe it is in God's hands and know that my healing is on its way God will get me through this storm for my anchor holds your anchor is Jesus he is with us every storm the word of God tells us a story of the wise men and Jesus sleeping on a boat the men was so scared on the sea they cried out Master Wake Up We Are Going To Die: there cry has awoken the master, the master is with you throughout your storm if you feel you have no faith and your scared wake up your master allow your cry to wake up your master. After church my face started to get worse after lunch my right side got so "week" I did not feel good at all so I went to the Hospital and everything just going all wrong no one could figure out what was wrong with me. It is bell palsy, no she is too young for that, it is not that she has a blood clot lets run some test nope no blood clot, she had a stroke nope no stroke, ok we are just going to guess give her medicine and be on our way, they said I have Conversion disorder gave me depression and anxiety medicine. Follow up with your doctor and you will be fine but we are keeping you for "couple" of days. I am laying there Monday night my I V hurting in my arm I pray Lord I want to go home this is so hard on my girls and they need me please let me go home tomorrow. The next day comes around and the doctor saw me and said you look so much better how do you feel? I feel so much better I want to go home, when can I go home? Dr said you can go home around 5:00 pm to day. I said okay. After I got home, I got to sleep in my bed and I had this dream I woke up on a boat and I was in this water with a bunch of sticks and black snakes with weird looking mouth and they would not bother me just floating down the stream. I woke up and it was morning I see this scripture my dad posted on

Face Book

My daughter Lavotus Sauceda is going through a physical trial.

My Daughter

Lord Your God

Isaiah 43: 1-4

43 But now, this is what the Lord says— he who created you, Jacob, he who formed you, Israel:

"Do not fear, for I have redeemed you;

I have summoned you by name; you are mine. 2 When you pass through the waters,

I will be with you;

and when you pass through the rivers, they will not sweep over you. When you walk through the fire, you will not be burned; the flames will not set you ablaze. 3 For I am the Lord your God, the Holy One of Israel, your Savior;

I give Egypt for your ransom, Cush[a] and Seba in your stead.

4 Since you are precious and honored in my sight, and because I love you,

That very next Sunday I saw a vision of a big foot while I was on that boat to step out and step on its head so I step out and I am following where he steps. That morning I got prayed for, and I felt healing in my mind and my, forehead was not tight any more. Each day my face would heal. People have faith in everything you do, God does not give up on us so we should not give up on our own self's we need to gain stronger to fight off the principalities the whiles of the darkness that surrounds us each day.

About a week later I saw my Dr. And he said your fine it's bell's palsy. I'm thinking to myself okay so what now? Dr said what did they give you in the ER? They said I have a Conversion Disorder.

Doctor said no you don't that's not what it is, he saw the pills in my hands and said this won't help you it won't do nothing for you, so he took me off the meds. 2 weeks later getting ready for camp meeting and the Lord told me I will defend you I will be your merical God every time.

Never mess with the Kings Daughter. Same with you Son or Daughter of the King tell your enemies Never Mess with the Kings Son or Daughter.

God healed me never ever give up your fight or your place in heaven keep fighting whatever fight whatever battle your up against God is with you walking every step of the way with you strengthening your armor your shield filling you up getting you ready for the race to overcome. SO OVER COME IT. YOU ARE CALLED TO BE AN OVER COMER.... You are also called to be victorious not a victim of this world.

So; I tell you be alive, allow the word of God Asunder to be alive in side of you to be and walk victorious you are a soldier of Christ stand tall and firm and be who God called and says for you to be.

When you get done with this book PLEASE don't keep it for yourself. Don't be selfish, pass it on to somebody else that you know who is going through a hard time. NO MATTER what it is give it to them as a gift lift somebody up who needs a miracle in their life. Someone who went through domestic abuse. Any one we all have a battle to face help so

Made in the USA
Columbia, SC
23 July 2020